Secondhand Lover

Secondhand Lover

A Brief Encounters Novella

Secondhand Lover
Published by Stacey Broadbent
Copyright © 2020 Cyan Tayse

Licence Notes

Proofreading and Editing by Spell Bound
Cover images from Deposit Photos

ISBN: 978-0-473-49360-8
          978-0-473-49361-5
          978-0-473-49362-2
          978-0-473-49363-9

A Note for the Reader

Grief hits people in different ways.
If you are grieving, whether from the death of a loved one, or perhaps even grieving the loss of a friendship or relationship, please don't be afraid to seek help. There is strength in asking for help.

And remember, be kind always. You never know what troubles someone is going through behind closed doors.

Chapter One

Orlando

"Brody, wait, don't leave like this." I stand on the doorstep, watching him pack his things into the boot of the car. "It doesn't have to be this way. I can change."

"Yes, it does, and no you can't." He slams the boot closed, turning to meet my eyes. "I'm sorry."

"Can't we at least try?" I take a step towards him, but he holds his hand up to stop me.

"Don't. It's better this way. You'll see." He rocks on his heels as he pulls his keys from his pocket. "I hope you find happiness, Lando." He ducks his head and walks around to the front of the car, climbing into the driver's seat. The car has barely had a chance to turn on before he pulls away from the curb.

"But I *was* happy with you." The words fall from my lips as I watch the taillights disappear around the corner. I continue staring at that same spot, hoping he'll change his mind and come back.

He doesn't.

Eighteen months. Eighteen months of my life I gave to him, and now I'm watching him walk out of my life for good. I know I'm not perfect, hell, I couldn't have been easy to live with while I was still grieving, but it was never my intention to make him feel like he was invisible. In fact, he was always the foremost thought on my mind at any given time. Apparently, that wasn't made obvious by my lack of conversation and head buried in my laptop. I know I have a tendency to get lost in my work, but writing a novel takes a lot of time and concentration, and when those words are flowing, you just don't want to stop. Fear of writer's block is a very real thing, and losing your muse can be crippling, so when it's there, you jump on it and go wherever it takes you, no matter the cost. It just so happens; my cost is my relationship with Brody.

How did I screw this up so badly? My book was meant to be a celebration of our love; a declaration, if you will. It was meant to be something I could put out into the world and announce, "He's mine, and I'm proud."

Now, it's more of a reminder of what could have been. A broken dream.

In hindsight, keeping it a secret probably wasn't my best idea. Maybe if I'd told him what I was doing, he'd have understood and hung around. Or maybe the breakup was imminent, and I was just too blind to see it. I guess I'll never know.

With the wind chilling my skin, I relent and go back inside; he's not coming back. Down the hall and to our... *my* room, I play over our earlier conversation.

"I've met someone."

"Like a therapist or something?" I say, *knowing full well what he meant.*

"No, Lando, like another man. I can't keep pretending everything is okay. You're never around, not really. You're always so lost in that damn book of yours, you don't even see what's going on around you."

"I didn't know you felt that way."

"No, well you wouldn't, would you? Not when you barely even look at me when I walk through the door. I got tired of being invisible, and Joshua... he sees me." He shrugs, taking my hand in his and giving a gentle squeeze. "You're still grieving, Lando, and that's okay. I can't imagine how hard this has been for you, but I need to look out for me, and right now, I need more than you can give. I'm sorry." Picking up his suitcase, he takes one last look around the room we shared for so long before walking towards the door.

"Why didn't you say anything before now? I could've tried harder, I would've." I sweep a hand across my head, gripping the muscles pulsing at the base of my neck. I want so much to reach out to him, to make him stay, but the look in his eyes tells me not to.

10

"No, you wouldn't have." He smiles wistfully. *"It's okay, Lando. I'm not mad at you. Not anymore. I just think we're too different."*

"And Joshua? He's not?"

"He's... he's what I need right now." He holds my stare for a beat before nodding his head towards the door. *"I've gotta go."*

"Just like that?"

"No point in dragging it out, is there?"

Standing at the entrance to my room, I can't bring myself to go in. Without his things, the room just seems bare and devoid of all emotion. His shoes no longer line the wall below the window – a habit that annoyed me to no end, but one I'd give almost anything to have back. The wardrobe door hangs open to show the empty hangers where his clothes used to be. On the duchess there's a gap where he kept his cologne and a framed picture of us. It's that gap that gets me the most. That empty space resonates with the gaping hole in my heart, and I can no longer hold in the tears as I crumple to the floor.

Cyan Tayse

Chapter Two

Stefan

"Where did you say you got this from?" I study the dark-haired teen who somehow managed to get his hands on a Fabergé egg. It wouldn't be the first time someone tried to fob off stolen goods in my store, but this is certainly the youngest one to try it.

"It was my grandmother's." He glances out the door then back to me. "She, uh, passed away."

"Right." I draw the word out as I nod. Pushing the egg aside, I rest my elbows on the counter. "Your friends put you up to this?"

"Wh-what? I don't know what you're talking about, man." He rakes his hand through his hair as he takes another look out the door.

"Are you gonna take it or not?" He shifts from one foot to the other.

"The thing is, I can get into a lot of trouble for buying and selling stolen goods." I raise a brow at him as I stand to my full height and fold my arms across my chest.

"I didn't steal it!" His voice cracks as he backs up. "I told you, it was my grandmother's."

"Mmmm." I nod again, unhinging the countertop so I can step through. "Fabergé eggs are priceless heirlooms. They're passed down through generations, and I doubt your grandmother, God rest her soul, would've wanted it to be sold in the local secondhand shop." I hold my hands up and shrug. "But that's just my opinion. I'm sure the cops would have another opinion on the subject."

"Shit," he hisses under his breath as he brings both hands up to grab the back of his neck. His eyes shift around the store as if looking for a way out, but I'm blocking the only exit. "Okay, I lied, Jesus! You can't get the cops involved, man, please."

Secondhand Lover

"You wanna tell me what you're really doing with a Fabergé egg that doesn't belong to you?"

"I, uh, found it?"

Squaring my shoulders, I pin him with a look. "Try again."

"Alright, alright." He brings his hands up in a defensive stance. "Keep your shirt on, man. I... I acquired it from a little old lady down the road." He nods towards downtown. "But I'll put it back, I swear, just don't call the cops, man, please. I won't do it again."

"How old are you, kid? Thirteen?"

"Fourteen." He puffs his chest out.

"What are you doing robbing old ladies? You need money, you go out there and get a job like the rest of us."

"I dunno." He shrugs. "Didn't look like she'd miss it. She has a bunch of 'em." He shakes his head. "I just wanted my brother to be happy again. He doesn't smile anymore. There's this book I wanted to get him, but I didn't have any cash." Blowing out a breath, he continues, "It was a dumb idea."

15

"Noble intentions, poorly executed, my friend." I clap a hand on his shoulder. "Look, I'm not going to call the cops, but I do need to talk to your parents. And then you and I are going to deliver this egg back to its rightful owner."

His brows shoot up. "Wh-what?"

"You heard me. You said you were gonna take it back, right? Well this way I can make sure you do."

"B-but she'll call the cops for sure!"

"You let me deal with that, okay?" I give his shoulder a squeeze. "Now, I'm gonna need your parents' number."

Chapter Three

Orlando

The knock on the door is expected, but knowing I have to pull myself together enough to be an adult when I can barely manage to haul my sorry butt out of bed in the morning makes it seem like a monumental task I'm not ready for.

Of all the days, why'd he pick today to get himself into trouble? Not that there's ever really a suitable time to get in trouble, or that tomorrow would've been any better. Or the next day, or the one after that for that matter. In all honesty, it's probably the push I need to drag myself back into the land of the living. I've had my time of wallowing in self-pity, now I need to front up and face the music, so to speak.

The knock comes again, only louder this time. I swipe a hand down my face as if the act will somehow wake me up and prepare me for what awaits behind that door.

"Lando, you there?" Gino's voice calls through the door. He sounds reserved, not at all like the carefree kid he usually is, and I blame myself for that. I know I haven't exactly been present the last week or so, maybe more, and with our parents no longer here, it's my responsibility to watch over him. It seems my relationship wasn't the only thing I let the ball drop on.

"Yeah, G, hang on." I force my feet to move down the hall. Two silhouettes show through the glass on the door, and even though I knew he was being accompanied home, it still sets my heart racing. I haven't had any adult interaction since Brody walked out the door three, or was it four weeks ago? The days are all blurring into one now, and aside from my brothers and their friends, I've conversed with no one. I shut myself away like a hermit crab, torturing myself by reading back through the declaration of love I'd been writing. The sad thing is, it's probably the best thing I've ever written, and now it's nothing more than a 70,000-word paperweight.

With the door handle in my grasp, I take a deep, calming breath. "Here goes," I whisper as I wrench the door open.

Gino stands there with his hands in his pockets and head down. Beside him is a man with dark hair and a touch of stubble on his chin. His leather jacket fits him like a second skin, and his jeans accentuate more than just his strong thighs.

"Orlando?" he asks, and I snap my eyes up to meet his. They're a shade of green I've never seen on any human before. Almost yellowish in colour, more like that of a cat, and I can't help but stare into them.

He clears his throat, holding his hand out to me. Blinking out of my trance, I quickly take his hand and give it a shake.

"Ah, yes, that's me. Thank you for bringing him back." I shift my gaze to Gino. "What'd you do?"

"I just wanted to do something nice for you, Lando." And just like that, I feel like an even bigger douchebag than I did before.

"Perhaps we could have a word in private?" Green eyes nods towards the lounge behind me.

"Ah, yeah, of course. Gino, why don't you go to your room while I talk to Mr... ah..." I flounder, realising I don't even know his name.

"Phillips, but you can call me Stefan. I don't feel old enough to be called Mr anything." He flashes me a smile, and for the first time in weeks, I get a flutter in my chest. Not the life-threatening kind of flutter either, the good kind that's both scary and exhilarating all at the same time.

Shaking my head at my body's reaction to this complete stranger, I lead him through to the kitchen, picking up stray items of clothing on the way. *Damn, when was the last time I opened the curtains in here?*

"Excuse the mess." I try to laugh to cover my embarrassment, but I'm not sure it

20

works. My face has always betrayed my emotions for all the world to see. My mother used to say it was the curse of a creative soul; wearing your feelings on the outside.

"Nothing I haven't seen before." He pulls out a seat at the breakfast bar, and I draw the blinds up to let in some light. Rays of sunshine cascade through the dusty glass, casting a sort of halo over the pile of dirty dishes in the sink, and I suck in a sharp breath as my heart stutters in my chest. The realisation of just how absent I've been of late sinks in, and I silently admonish myself as I set about making some coffee with the only clean cups left in the cupboard.

Turning to Stefan with a sheepish smile, I offer a weak excuse. "It really isn't normally this messy. You caught me on an off day."

He doesn't say anything, but he doesn't have to. His eyes speak volumes as they search mine, and under his scrutiny, I feel almost naked. Needing to catch my breath, I wiggle the cups in the air. "How do you take your coffee?"

"Black, no sugar, thanks."

"Sweet enough already," I say before I can stop myself. My eyes widen and I quickly spin away from him, ducking my head and closing my eyes as I try to gather myself. I don't miss the light chuckle that comes from behind me.

"So they tell me." His knuckles rap against the counter in a tune as he sits, and for some reason that puts me at ease. Still, I keep my back to him until I'm sure my cheeks have returned to their usual hue.

When I hand Stefan his coffee, his eyes search mine again, as if he can't quite figure me out. Placing his cup on the counter, he rakes a hand through his hair. "I'm sorry, I'm trying to work out the dynamic here. You don't look old enough to have a teen. You are who I spoke to on the phone?"

"Ah yeah, sorry, I thought Gino would've explained." My eyes find the framed picture hanging above the mantle, the one where everyone is happy and *alive.* "Our parents died in a car accident a few years ago."

Secondhand Lover

Stefan follows my gaze, his head nodding gently. "Sorry for your loss. That must've been hard." He turns back, his fingers stretching forward, but not enough to make contact.

"It was. I was only nineteen, and suddenly I had two kid brothers to raise." I shrug. "But you do what you have to. Family, ya know?"

"For sure. Still, it's a lot for a nineteen-year-old to take on. Did you have any support? Anyone to help you? I mean, at nineteen you're still just a kid yourself." He takes a sip of his coffee, his eyes boring into mine. I can't tell whether or not to be offended at the suggestion I wasn't mature enough to handle my brothers. It wasn't easy, not by a long shot, but I think I've done all right by them. At least, I thought I had up until now.

"We do all right." My gaze falls to the cup in my hand as my thumb trails the rim.

"Hey." His hand stretches out, the tips of his fingers brushing the back of my hand. "I didn't mean anything by it. Gino seems like a good kid."

I lift my eyes to meet his. "He is. He's a great kid." Closing my eyes, I tilt my head back with a sigh. "I haven't been paying attention lately. I've been... distracted."

"We all get distracted. It's part of being human." He takes a breath and his eyes soften. "He mentioned wanting you to be happy again?"

I don't know what I was expecting him to say, but it wasn't that. Have I really been that miserable that my kid brother would tell a complete stranger he wants me to be happy again? Jesus.

Bringing my hand up to pinch the bridge of my nose, I shake my head. "I didn't realise he felt that way." The words are barely more than a whisper. "I know I haven't been myself, but I thought... I don't know." I look towards Gino's room as my eyes fill with tears. "I thought I was hiding it better."

Chapter Four

Stefan

I feel for the guy. Whatever he's going through has knocked him for a six, and I can see how hard he's trying to keep it together for his younger brothers. If only he could see the strength he has inside. Not every nineteen-year-old could easily take on the role of parent while also grieving. That takes something special.

"It's okay if you're not okay." I nod my head towards the closed door in the hallway. "That kid in there just wants to help you. He can see you're hurting."

"It's not his job to help me." He points a finger out the door, and I can see the effort it's taking for him to hold in the tears. "He's been through enough already. It's my job to protect him, not the other way around." He shakes his head. "No twelve-year-old should have to bury their parents."

"No child, period, should have to do that. I get that you had to step up, but *you* had to bury your parents too. I'm guessing you didn't get a chance to really grieve yourself either."

He juts his chin out. "I grieved in my own way."

I can see where Gino gets his stubborn nature from. Perhaps I'm coming at this the wrong way.

"Look, I didn't come here to lecture you or tell you how to parent, and I get the feeling you don't really want to talk, so I'll get down to business and keep this brief." I lean back in my seat, pursing my lips. "I run the secondhand shop down on South Street, *Seconds Away*, and Gino tried to sell me something he'd stolen from a little old lady."

"He what?" His eyebrows shoot up as he grips the back of his neck – a trait the two brothers share.

I hold my hands up to placate him. "I've sorted it out already. He and I went down to pay Mrs. Sanders a visit, and he apologised for what he did. I had a word with her, and she's happy to let me handle it instead of going to the police seeing as he's so young. And to be honest, I could tell it wasn't something he would usually do."

"Jesus." Orlando paces from the kitchen sink to the cupboard and back again. "Why would he do that?"

I know he's not really expecting an answer, but I give him one anyway. "He wanted to get you something and he had no money."

"He… Oh my god." Tears fill his eyes as he frowns. "This is all my fault."

Pushing up from my seat, I round the breakfast bar and take hold of his shoulders. "This is *not* your fault. Yes, you've been distracted, as you said, but he's a good kid, and he knew what he was doing was wrong. This is not on you."

"How can you say that? If I hadn't been wallowing, he wouldn't have had any reason to do that." His eyes keep flicking around the room, looking everywhere but at me.

"He's fourteen. He knows right from wrong. And to be honest, I think this is probably the scare he needs to make sure he doesn't go down that road." I duck my head to try and catch his gaze. "Okay?"

He gives a small nod, but I can see he has his doubts. "What do we do now?"

"That's why I'm here, actually. Like I said, I don't believe he's a bad kid, he's just trying to do the right thing in the wrong way." I pull some papers from my back pocket and place them on the counter. "I'd like to offer him a job."

"You what? You can't be serious."

"It's all here in black and white." I pat the contract. "I'd like him to work in the shop three afternoons a week so he can *earn* his money. He can start tomorrow if that's okay with you. Mrs. Sanders would like him to mow her lawns for her too."

28

He picks up the contract and skims it. "Why are you doing this?"

I lean my hip against the counter and fold my arms across my chest. "I believe in second chances. And after meeting you, I can see that it would do you some good too, give you a little breathing space."

"But you don't even know us, and Gino could've got you in trouble with what he did. Why do you even care?"

"Because once upon a time, I was a kid like Gino, and someone offered me a second chance."

Cyan Tayse

Chapter Five

Orlando

"Just think about it," he says, tapping his finger on the papers again. "I'll swing by tomorrow morning to pick Gino up and take him around to see Mrs. Sanders. You can let me know then."

"You don't have to—"

He holds his hand up to stop me. "I know I don't. But I want to." His smile is genuine, but it doesn't stop the sting of pride inside. We're not some charity case who can't get by without the help from a kindly stranger, no matter how attractive he is.

"Tell me if I'm stepping out of line here, but... if you ever need someone to talk to..." he opens his arms out, palms up, "...I'm a pretty good listener."

"Thanks, but I'm okay, really." I plaster a smile on my face to prove it.

"Well, the offer's there if you change your mind." Stepping backwards, he hooks a thumb over his shoulder. "I'd better get back to the shop. I'll leave you to think it over."

My hand reaches out of its own accord, and I push off the counter. "Thanks… for being so cool about it all and bringing him back. I know you didn't have to do that."

"It was my pleasure. Like I said, I can tell he's a good kid. He just needs a little guidance."

I walk him to the front door, holding it open as he steps through. "Well, um, I guess I'll see you tomorrow then?"

"Bright and early." He grins, sliding his shades on and hiding those brilliant eyes of his. "See ya then." He waves as he walks down the path to his car, and I stand there gawking at him like a lovesick teenager.

How can a man I've only just met have such an impact on me? I keep swinging from infatuation to sheer embarrassment and

Secondhand Lover

mortification. With a shake of my head, I raise my hand in a final wave as he pulls away from the curb. Perhaps it's time I stop hiding in my room and venture out into the world again.

"How much trouble am I in?" Gino stands behind me with his head hanging low and his hands in his pockets, and I'm reminded of the first time I ever got in big trouble with Mum and Dad. One of my favourite authors had come to town for a book signing, and I'd cut class to see him. I hadn't counted on my parents being there to surprise me with a signed copy. The look of disappointment on their faces was worse than any punishment they could dole out. I was one of those straight-A students who never stepped out of line, and I most definitely didn't cut classes, especially when those classes were actually end of year exams and important for getting into university.

Of course, those dreams died alongside my parents. I'd barely started my first year at Lincoln when they had their accident and I had to come back home to take care of everything.

33

My brothers became my sole priority, and I vowed never to disappoint them the way I disappointed my parents.

With a sigh, I rake my hand through my hair then wrap it around the back of his neck, pulling him into my chest. "G, I'm sorry for letting you down these past few weeks. I didn't realise how removed I was." I pull back to look into his eyes. "Let's make a deal. I'll try harder to be more present, and you won't go knocking off any old ladies, capiche?"

He nods, a sly smile forming on his lips. "So, I'm not in trouble then?"

"Oh, you're in trouble. Starting tomorrow, you'll be helping out Mrs. Sanders with her yard, and then Stefan wants you to work in his store." His smile drops and a frown mars his face. "For money. He's offering you a job, and I think you should take it." The words surprise me just as much as they do Gino, but deep down, I know it's the right decision. We're not a charity case, but I can swallow my pride for Gino. It'll be good for him.

Chapter Six

Stefan

"Two flat whites, please." I hold up two fingers with a grin. "And throw in four of those croissants too, please." Opening my wallet, I pull out a fifty and hand it to Sandy with a wink. "You can keep the change."

"Mr. Phillips, you don't have to do that." She rings up my order and holds the change out to me.

"We've been over this, Sandy. It's Stefan, and I want to." I fold her fingers back over the cash and nod towards her rounded belly. "It's only a matter of time before you'll have your hands full, so treat yourself to something sweet on your break, I insist."

A blush colours her cheeks as she pockets the change with a nod of thanks, and I lift my cup in a salute as I walk out the door.

I've been a regular at *Roasted Beans* for my morning coffee since they opened their doors two years ago. Not only is it handy to *Seconds Away*, it's also the best coffee in town. Sandy runs the boutique coffee shop with her husband, Brett, and you can tell they've put their heart and soul into the place. It's always bustling with customers, and the atmosphere is inviting. Nothing like those giant conglomerates that only care about the bottom line. I guess that's why I love this community so much; it's full of honest to goodness people just trying to make their mark and earn a living while they're at it. My kind of people.

The drive to pick up Gino is short, and for reasons I can't explain, it has my stomach all in knots. Sure, I'm taking a risk on this kid, but it's not him I'm worried about; it's his brother. Orlando has the look of someone who's been hurt one too many times. A look I'm all too familiar with.

Like Orlando, I too lost my parents at a young age, only I didn't have a big brother to step in and look after me. Too old to be adopted, and too young to live on my own, I got lost in the system. Bouncing around from foster home to foster home where they were really only interested in the money they received from the government to care for me, if that's what you could call it, I quickly learned how to shut up and keep to myself.

I was sixteen when I took matters into my own hands and took off into the night. Sleeping under bridges or behind dumpsters down alleyways became my norm, and I spent my days wandering the streets in search of money and food.

Six months of sleeping rough, and I was on my last legs. Curled in a ball, with my sleeping bag around me and a makeshift roof made of a carboard box, I knew my days were numbered. Too weak to venture out and look for food, too proud to beg. It was then a kindly stranger pulled up beside me in a beat-up old jeep. Mr. Reynolds had a weathered face and crooked teeth, but his eyes were kind. He picked me up off the street and offered me a place to stay in exchange for help on the farm. I didn't have the strength to fight him, so I went. It was the best thing that ever happened to me. He showed me the value of a hard day's work, and that no matter how little you have, you can always spare a moment of kindness.

Not a day goes by I don't think of Mr. Reynolds and all he did for me over the years. I lost one of the best friend's I've ever had the day he died, but I know he'd be watching over me right now with a smile on his face. Kindness above all else.

I pull up outside Orlando's, grab the coffees and pastries, then head up the path to the door. Gino greets me, taking the croissants off my hands as he leads me through to the kitchen.

An electric charge fills the air as I meet Orlando's gaze. He seems different today, brighter. I hold up the coffees with a grin. "I brought breakfast. There's this little shop down the road that makes the best coffees." I place the holder down on the counter, taking a cup out and handing it to him. "One flat white."

"Thanks. You didn't have to do that." He takes the cup, his fingers brushing against mine.

"He got these too." Gino holds up the bag of croissants, one already in his hand with a bite taken out. "They're really good."

"G, did you even ask before helping yourself?" Orlando scolds, and I can't help but chuckle.

"It's fine, honestly. I got one for each of us. Your brother too if he's here." I take the bag from Gino and rip it open further, taking one for myself and pushing the bag towards Orlando. "They hand make them every morning. It's impossible to pass them up."

"Hey, Mario!" Gino calls down the hallway. "If you don't get your butt outta bed, I'm gonna eat your breakfast!" He grins, shoving another piece of bread into his mouth. "I'm not even joking."

He practically inhales the rest and eyes up the last one on the counter. Orlando slides it away from him and puts it on a plate. "I'm putting this aside for Mario. You've had enough, G."

"Aww, come on, Lando. I've gotta keep my strength up for the yard work I'm doing today."

His brother leans back, folding his arms across his chest. "Mmhmm. And *why* is it you're doing yard work again?" He taps a finger against his chin. "Oh, that's right, because you took something that didn't belong to you."

Gino's face drops and he kicks a foot against the carpet. "Yeah, yeah, I know."

Orlando rounds the corner to rough up his hair. "I know you do. Now, go wash up. Make yourself presentable." He turns to me with wide eyes. "Sorry about that. You'd think he doesn't get fed around here." He chuckles, picking up his coffee. "Really though, thanks for all this. You didn't have to do that. We have food here."

"Oh, no I know. Like I said, I stop there every morning for a coffee, and I couldn't resist the pastries." I rub a hand over my stomach with a laugh. "Though I probably should."

"Pfft, hardly." His eyes dart up to mine and back down to stare at his cup with scrutiny, as if he can find the very meaning of life in the moulded plastic lid.

His compliment sends warmth through me, and though I'm sure he's regretting the slip, I'm certainly not. I don't recall the last time anyone looked at me the way Orlando does when he's not trying to hide, and I'm not ashamed to say I like it. I like it a whole lot.

Cyan Tayse

Chapter Seven

Orlando

Three cups of coffee and two hours of my day, and still no words will come. I've been staring at the blinking cursor the whole time, willing inspiration to hit. I may have told Stefan we have food here, but the cupboards are looking awfully sad and bare right about now. If we're going to eat this week, I need to get something to my editor by the end of the day. *Truly You* goes to print every Thursday morning, and cut-off for submissions is midnight tonight. Thankfully, I have an understanding boss. I've been a walking shadow these past few weeks, and it's time I got myself back out there again, if only to show Gino he doesn't need to worry.

"Hey, Lando." One of my brother's friends leans against the doorframe, his arms folded across his chest. "You doin' okay?" Of all the kids Mario gets around with, Leo is my favourite. He's got a good heart, and like me, he's had to raise his kid brother. Only difference is his mum is still around.

"Yeah, man. I'm doin' okay." And for the first time in a long time, I know I'm not lying. I really *do* feel more like myself. "How's things at home? Your mum…"

He runs a hand down his face. "She's trying, so that's something." He nods at the laptop in front of me. "You working on your next bestseller?"

My eyes roll so hard I can see the wall behind me. "I wish. Just trying to come up with something to write for tomorrow's issue. Writer's block." I shake my head. "It sure is a buzzkill."

Leo chuckles. "I'm sure you'll think of something. You always do."

"Not lately, I don't. I can't seem to get outta my own head, ya know?" I wave my hand at the pile of papers on the floor. "I wasted so much time writing something that'll never see the light of day, and now it's like I'm sucked dry."

"It'll come to you. Maybe get outta here for a bit. Go for a walk around the block or something. That's what Alex always does."

Pushing the lid down on the laptop, I nod. "Yeah, you're probably right." A burst of laughter comes from down the hall. "What're you lot doing here anyway? Shouldn't you be out enjoying the summer holidays?"

"We will. Alex wanted to share his news with the guys first." He grins, pride shining in his eyes.

"He got the scholarship?"

"Yes, sir, he did. Like I knew he would."

An unwanted pang of jealousy hits, but I swipe it away and plaster a smile on my face. "That's fantastic. He deserves to have some good in his life."

A shadow crosses Leo's face as he pushes off the wall, and I know he's thinking about the night Alex came out to his father. If

Leo hadn't been there... It doesn't bear thinking about.

"He does. We all do." He holds my gaze for a beat. "You know, you could always go back. It's not too late."

My head is shaking before he even finishes speaking. "Nah, I have responsibilities here. It's not my time." I push the laptop aside and get to my feet. "Tell Alex congratulations from me, though. I'm happy for him."

He purses his lips but doesn't say anything, just nods and turns back down the hall. Mario tried telling me the same thing, but I can't leave him and Gino to their own devices. As much as I'd like to believe Mario gets his money on the up and up, something in my gut tells me otherwise. What kind of security company hires a seventeen-year-old kid to install their home security system? It just doesn't add up. He's a smart one, though. Always has been. And he's damn good at covering his tracks. I've looked up the company, and they seem legit, but something about it doesn't wash with me, and I'll be damned if I let Gino get into something like that. He's a good kid, but he doesn't have the same street smarts Mario does.

Speak of the devil. "Hey, we're gonna head into Mickey D's for some burgers to celebrate Alex being accepted..." Mario clears his throat, glancing behind him before continuing. "Sorry, bro. You wanna come with?" He hooks a thumb over his shoulder.

"Thanks, but I'm good. You go though." I pull my wallet out of my back pocket. "You need any money? I don't have much but..." I hold out a crumpled ten dollar note, but he waves it off.

"Nah, man, I'm good. Keep it." He holds his palm up, the other hand rubbing across it like he's dishing out dollars at the club. "I'm making bank, son."

I raise a questioning brow at him. "When did you become an American gangster?"

He straightens. "I'm just playin', you know that."

"Are you though?"

"What's that supposed to mean?" He squares his shoulders. "What are you trying to say, Lando?"

I pull him further into the room, away from prying eyes. "You know your brother got caught trying to sell stolen goods to a store just down the road yesterday?"

His eyes widen, and he shoves his hands in his pockets, rocking back on his heels. "Shit. Nah, man, I didn't know."

"You didn't…"

"Didn't what? School him? Shit, Lando, you think I'd do that to my baby brother?"

I rake my hand through my hair, gripping the base of my neck with a sigh. "No. I don't."

"Good, 'cause everyone knows you don't shit in your own backyard. That's a rookie move." He grins then darts out the door with his friends in tow.

Chapter Eight

Stefan

I have to admit, the kid's a good worker. He did a great job on Mrs. Sanders' yard, and he's spent the rest of the afternoon with me, wiping down the counter and everything in the cabinet beneath. In fact, he'd probably still be doing it if I hadn't dragged him out and locked the door behind us.

"How does it feel to do an honest day's work?" I glance at him sitting beside me in the car. Aside from this morning, he's barely said boo all day, and I don't know if that's a good thing or not.

"Alright, I guess." He shrugs, staring out the window. "How much longer do I have to keep working with you?"

"Ouch." I hold a fist against my chest. "You saying you didn't get a kick out of all that cleaning you did today?"

The hint of a smile graces his lips, but he quickly schools his expression, rolling his eyes with a snort. "Yeah, I just *love* to clean all day."

"Excellent! Wait 'til you see what I have for you to do on Friday." I grin, waggling my eyebrows at him.

"Friday?" he whines. "Dude, it's the holidays. Do I have to come in so often?"

"Yeah, *dude*, you do. That's how a job works. People work hard each and every day to pay for those nice things that you thought you were entitled to." I pin him with a look, and he shifts uncomfortably.

"I know, okay? I know what I did was stupid and wrong. You don't have to keep on at me about it." He holds his hands up, shaking them as he puts on a voice. "You do the crime, you do the time. I get it." He folds his arms across his chest and slumps further down in his seat.

I pull the car up outside his house then turn to face him. "Look, kid, I know you think this whole thing is unfair and your brother and I are being hard on you, but that's the way the world works I'm afraid. For every action there is a consequence, and you have to be prepared to face whatever those consequences are. Yeah, you might've had a noble idea in your head when you did it, but you knew it was wrong and you chose to do it anyway." I take a breath, staring up at the house for a moment. "You said yourself, you wanted to make Orlando smile again, so don't you think you owe it to him to see this through?"

Gino rakes a hand through his hair as he huffs out a breath. "Yeah, I guess so." He opens the door and steps out onto the path before leaning back through the window. "I really am sorry for what I did."

"I know you are, but that's exactly why you have to stick it out. Show Orlando you're trying."

He nods. "Okay. I will. You coming in?"

51

I'd be lying if I said I didn't want to see Orlando again, it's whether he wants to see me though. Whatever it was that made him close himself off is obviously still fresh, and I'd hate to impose more than I already have. "Uh... I don't know." I check my watch for want of something to do.

"I just..." he glances back towards the house then lowers his head further through the window, "... I think he really likes you. He was different after you left last night. Kinda like the old him again." He shrugs, pulling up to stand. "But whatever."

My heart shouldn't kick at the mention of him liking me, but it does, and even though I know I shouldn't, I climb out of the car and follow him up to the house. *Just one coffee then I'll go.*

Gino opens the door, calling out as he saunters down the hall. "Lando, I'm home! Stefan is here too!"

There's a muttered curse followed by the thud of something being placed on a desk. Orlando sticks his head around the corner from further down the hall. "I'll be there in a sec, just make yourself at home." He waves a hand towards the kitchen, so I give him a nod and make my way through. Gino follows me, filling the jug and switching it on before heading back to his room with a wink. *This kid.*

"Sorry about that, just had to save my article before I lost it again." Orlando swipes a hand through his hair and down to grip the base of his neck. "Technology can be a godsend one minute and a hindrance the next, I tell ya."

"What are you working on?" I ask as I take a seat at the counter, watching him make coffee.

"Oh, just a puff piece really." He waves a hand through the air as if it's nothing. "I haven't really ventured out much lately, so I haven't had my ear to the ground, so to speak. But we've got bills to pay, so…" He clears his throat, turning to face me with a shake of his head. "Never mind. You don't want to hear about that. How did it go today?" He nods his head in Gino's direction. "Was he good?"

"He was. Mrs. Sanders was happy with the yard work, and he's spent the better half of the day cleaning out cabinets." I lean back in my seat, a smile playing across my face. "I don't think he enjoyed it too much, but he's coming back Friday, so…" I open my arms out as if to say, we'll see.

"Are you sure you don't mind? I can find some work for him to do around here as punishment so he's not in your hair." His eyes scan the room, searching for possible jobs.

"It's really no bother. He doesn't talk much, but it's nice to have the company. And I think if he gave it a chance, he'd realise it's not so bad working for his money."

"Hmm, I hope so."

"He will, you'll see." I tap the counter, trying to think of something to keep the conversation going. "So, you write?" I peer at him over my coffee cup. "Would I have read anything you've written?"

"Oh, no, probably not." Again he waves his hand dismissively, as if he's not any good. "I write for *Truly You* magazine. It's not what I'd like to be doing full time, but I can do it from home and still be here when the boys need me. The pay's pretty good when I can actually get my head around the writer's block." He chuckles, the sound warm and inviting.

"Wow. I can't write to save myself. I bet that's a fulfilling job; telling the stories that need to be told." The more I get to know this guy, the more awed I am with him. Not only has he raised his kid brothers, he's secured himself a job with one of the major magazines in the area. That's impressive for someone so young.

He laughs again. "I don't know that I'd go that far. Like I said, it's a puff piece, not cutting-edge journalism."

"So, what would you like to be writing about?"

His cheeks redden as he stares into his coffee cup. "I don't really want to be a journalist. I kinda stumbled into it when I had to step up and look after Mario and Gino, but fiction is where my heart is. I was attending Lincoln, doing my BA and majoring in literature when our parents died. I had grand plans to write the greatest romance novel of our time." He smiles, lifting his gaze to meet mine. "I know that sounds silly, but growing up, there weren't any stories for people like me. No one wrote about two men falling in love, and I don't know." He shrugs. "Maybe if more stories had been written about the beauty of it, there wouldn't have been such a stigma around being gay or bi or whatever."

I reach out and take his hand before I can stop myself. "It's not silly at all. I think it's a great idea. What's stopping you?"

"Huh." He drags his gaze from mine, instead looking out towards the front door. "I *was* writing something, but I let it take over and, in the end, I pushed away the person I was writing it for."

It all makes sense now. *He* hasn't been broken; his heart has. "Okay, but what happened to writing for you?"

He turns to me, his brows furrowed and his mouth opening and closing as if he can't quite think of the words to say. "I think maybe I lost sight of that."

I nod. "Maybe you need to revisit it."

He shakes his head. "I can't."

"I know it can't be easy to write a love story when your heart is broken, but that's why you *have* to do it. Write the story *you* needed to read growing up. Write for the boy who felt ashamed of who he was. Finish the story and give it the ending you hoped for." Moving to stand in front of him, I stroke a finger down his cheek before pressing my lips to his in a soft kiss. "Because it's in there." I touch my palm against his chest. "It's in you, in me, in all of us. Write what's in your heart."

Cyan Tayse

Chapter Nine

Orlando

He kissed me.
Stefan kissed me.
What does that even mean?

He left twenty minutes ago, and still his kiss lingers on my lips. A kiss meant to inspire and encourage, but one I won't soon forget. Stefan was a stranger to me only yesterday, but somehow, he sees inside my soul, more than Brody ever did the entire time we were together. Perhaps what I thought was love, was merely infatuation and nothing more, because if it was love, surely the kiss of a stranger wouldn't strike me breathless as this has.

I stare up at the ceiling, my mind racing with so many ideas. Maybe he's right. Maybe I should finish the story, or better yet, start afresh. I am a writer. My mind is the creator of worlds and wonderment. I may not have found my one true love or lived the greatest love story of the ages, but I have lived a life of love all the same.

My parents, though unaware of my sexuality, would've supported me regardless, of that I'm sure. I don't know why I never told them. I guess I didn't feel I had to; I just knew they wouldn't care either way. They had the kind of relationship you admire and aspire to have, and they made damn sure we knew how loved and wanted we were too. I miss them so much it hurts sometimes, and I guess Stefan was right when he suggested I never really had the chance to grieve for them properly, what with being thrown into parenthood so quickly. That in itself has taught me so much about love. I mean, they're my brothers so obviously I already loved them, but when you become responsible for another human being it changes things. It puts things into perspective, I guess. Suddenly your needs aren't as important, and you find yourself doing anything you can to make *their* lives better. At least, that's what I thought I had been doing until yesterday.

Man, I really dropped the ball there. And not just with Gino. I've let Mario do as he pleases, and deep down, I know everything isn't above board there, but he's never given me any trouble, so I let it slide. Of course, there's Brody too. We had a good thing going for a while there, and even if it wasn't truly love, it meant the world to me at the time. Maybe it was my way of coping with a loss I was in no way prepared for, or maybe it was never meant to be in the first place. One thing I do know, though, is it led me down the path I'm on now. A path I didn't see coming until it smacked me in the face.

Little by little, Stefan is breaking down those barriers I've had up since I was nineteen. He's making me *feel* again, and he's awakened something inside of me. Something I thought I'd never get back; hope.

Cyan Tayse

Chapter Ten

Stefan

I don't know what came over me. I never should have kissed him like that. The poor guy is struggling with a breakup and dealing with his kid brothers, and I come waltzing in there, complicating things. Yes, I'm attracted to him, but now isn't the time. In fact, it may never be the time. He has so much on his plate right now, and I'd be a fool to think I could simply slot myself into his life. Or is that what I've been trying to do all along? He didn't ask for my help, in fact, he was pretty adamant he could handle the situation on his own. So, why did I feel the need to jump in there and rescue him?

Because you like him.

And I do. I like him a whole lot. Way more than I probably should, because he's in no position to reciprocate those feelings. He was writing a romance about the last guy he was with for God's sake, if that doesn't scream unavailable, I don't know what does.

Still, the look on his face as I walked away wasn't one of distaste. No, there was the tiniest hint of a smile on those lips of his, and a rosy colouring to his cheeks. If I didn't know any better, I'd think he enjoyed it as much as I did. But I do know better, and there's no way I can start something with him right now, not when he's in a healing stage. What I can do though is be there for him, because what I see when I look at him, is someone struggling to find themselves. In the few conversations we've had he's made it clear that his needs don't matter, and he's put everyone else ahead of himself. If I can do one thing for him, I hope it's to make him see how truly amazing he is.

An idea forms in my mind, one that, if it works, could show him just how much potential he has. It could show him that *his* dreams matter too and it's okay to pursue them. Or it could backfire and send him running in the opposite direction.

I think back to a time when Mr. Reynolds was still around, and I know without a doubt what he would tell me to do. Even though I risk the chance of Orlando turning his back on me, I have to at least try. If anyone deserves a bit of kindness in their life, it's him.

I'm picking Gino up again on Friday, so that gives me all of tomorrow to do a bit of research before I make my move.

Cyan Tayse

Chapter Eleven

Orlando

The minute I hear his car pull up, my heart starts racing. I push aside my laptop and head out to the kitchen, trying not to seem too eager to see him.

"Stefan's here." Gino saunters through from his room with a smile on his face.

"You seem awfully happy for someone who didn't want to go to work." I fill the sink with water and detergent, ready to tackle the dishes on the counter.

"I don't know." He shrugs. "Stefan is pretty cool." There's a knock on the door, and he backs towards it. "Plus, I like the way you are when he's around." He turns on his heels and runs to the door, leaving me breathless.

The way I am when he's around? I stare into the sink full of dishes, letting that thought sink in for a moment. Have I really changed so much since he's been coming to visit? Looking around the room no longer plunged in a constant state of darkness and filth, it's obvious I have.

"Afternoon, boys. I stopped by the coffee shop on my way over. Thought we could have a bite to eat before G here helps me out at the store." Stefan grins as he places two steaming coffees on the counter and a bag of savouries. "I wasn't sure what you like, so I grabbed a few of each."

Gino tears into the bag, pulling out a pinwheel and shoving the whole thing into his mouth. "It's so good."

Drying my hands on a dishtowel, I lean against the counter, letting my eyes rove over Stefan. His broad shoulders shake as he laughs, watching Gino devour half the pastries in a matter of seconds.

"Woah there, slow down. You'll give yourself indigestion."

He leans across to swipe the bag out of Gino's reach, and as he does, his elbow knocks one of the coffees. The lid pops off and hot coffee splatters over his clean, *white* shirt.

"Oh, shit!" He jumps up, holding his hands like a cup to catch the dripping coffee as it spills over the counter. "Sorry. Have you got a cloth to clean this up?"

I throw the dishtowel still in my hands, and quickly wet a sponge for his shirt. As he soaks up the mess on the counter, I dab the sponge against his abdomen. The muscles ripple with every move he makes, and the room suddenly feels extremely hot.

"God, I can be such a klutz sometimes. Sorry." He drops to his knees to mop the carpet.

"It's fine, Stefan, really." I crouch beside him, taking the cloth. "Just leave it. It's your shirt I'm more worried about." I wince at the brown stain covering his middle. "I hope it wasn't expensive."

"This old thing?" He pulls the sopping-wet fabric from his torso. "I don't suppose you

69

have something I could borrow while I'm at work?"

"Of course! Here, you can choose something from my closet, and I'll get that washed and ready for you when you drop Gino back tonight." I lead him down the hall and to my room, the butterflies in my stomach doing a jig. I have to remind myself he's just borrowing a shirt, nothing more.

"Here you go." I fling the closet open and step back, my eyes landing on his bare chest. "Oh.*" Stefan is standing in my bedroom without a shirt on.* In fact, he's using his shirt to dab at his stomach, and my God, the way his abs flex under his hand, it's almost criminal.

"Do you mind if I use your bathroom to get this stickiness off too please?" His eyes meet mine, and all I can do is nod because it's taking all my effort to keep my tongue in my mouth and not lolling out.

He holds my stare until the corners of his mouth lift and he chuckles, snapping me out of it. "Oh, right. I'll uh, leave you to it then."

I dart around him and out the door, making my way back to the kitchen, where I lean my back against the wall and close my eyes, sucking in air.

"You okay, bro?" I open my eyes to see Gino grinning at me. "You look a little flustered."

"Shut up, I'm fine." I push away from the wall and head back to the dishes, my heart slowly returning to normal. I bite my lip in an attempt to keep it in place, but I can't help the smile that fights its way through.

Chapter Twelve

Stefan

I don't have much time. Throwing my shirt into the laundry hamper, I grab the first clean shirt I see and throw it on while pulling open drawers as quietly as I can. Aside from neatly folded clothes and a drawer full of toiletries, there's nothing I'm looking for. There doesn't appear to be a desk out in the living area, and his laptop is on his bed, so this is clearly where he works, but where does he keep what he's written? There has to be a notebook or something I can use.

With a quick glance out the door, I drop to my hands and knees and lift the duvet from the floor to peer under the bed; nothing. I go back to the closet in case there was a box I missed, but it's all clothes and shoes. I'm about ready to give up when I spy a pile of papers shoved between the bed and the drawers on the other side of the room.

I peel the first few pages away and instantly I can tell this is the story he was talking about; the one he wrote for his ex. I know he said he wasn't ready to share it, and perhaps he never will be, but with little else to use, I'm left with no choice. I pull out my phone and snap some shots of the pages. Just a few. Just enough to show how good it is. And it is. My God it's good. I know I shouldn't be reading it, that's not what I came here for, but the first few words on the page draw me in, and I can't tear my eyes away. Perching on the edge of the bed, I devour the words in front of me, feeling every bit of emotion he's poured onto those pages. It's even better than I imagined it would be, and I wish there was more time for me to read the whole thing.

"What are you doing?" Orlando's voice comes from behind me, and I just about jump out of my skin. I'd been so engrossed in what I was reading I hadn't heard him come in. The pages crumple in my hand as I spin to face him, and a look of horror crosses his face. His eyes flick from the pages to my face and back again.

"I'm sorry, Orlando. I should've asked first, but this is—"

"Private," he interrupts, stalking around the bed and snatching the papers from my hand. "I told you it's not finished."

"I know, and I'm sorry." I stand, reaching out to him, but he backs away. "It's really good, Orlando. Like *really* good." I rake my hand through my hair. "You should publish it."

"What makes you the expert? You said yourself, you can't write to save yourself, so how would you know if it was any good?" His whole body shakes with anger as he steps closer. "You had no right to read this." He waves the papers in the air as tears fill his eyes. His shoulders droop, and the anger disappears from his face, replaced with something much worse; pain. "No right." His hand drops and he stares out the window, shaking his head. "It wasn't for you to read," he whispers, and my chest tightens. I'm not sure I can follow through with it now. Not when he looks so… broken.

"I should go," I say, but I don't move from my spot. I need him to look at me, to show me he's okay. That *we're* okay.

"That's probably best." He folds his arms across his chest and steps aside, his eyes focused on something out the window. Something other than me.

With shaking fingers, I button up the shirt I borrowed and slip past him. Stopping at the door, I turn but he's still facing away from me. "I really am sorry. Sorry that I didn't ask first, but not sorry that I read it. It's a shame for it to be shoved in the corner of your room instead of out there in the world for all to see." I pause, waiting for a response that never comes. Dropping my head, I step out into the hall. "I hope you can forgive me."

Chapter Thirteen

Orlando

The second I hear the front door close, I let the pages fall to the floor as my legs buckle beneath me. Catching myself on the corner of the bed, I bury my face in the sheets and yell. I yell until my throat hurts and my voice is hoarse.

"Lando?"

I lift my head to see Mario standing half in the doorway and half in the hall, as if he can't quite decide what to do or where to be. Sniffing, I pull myself together, pushing up off the floor. "I'm okay."

"Like hell you are. What happened?"

"It doesn't matter."

"Would you just stop already?" Mario slaps his hand against the doorframe then stalks into the room. "We're not these poor defenseless little kids like you think, Lando. You don't have to protect us from everything."

"I know you're not little kids anymore. I know that. But the day Mum and Dad died…" my voice cracks and I have to take a breath. "The day they died, you became my responsibility. It's my *job* to look after you two."

"And what about you? Who looks after you? Because it sure as shit ain't you." He pauses, raking his hand through his hair. "Mum and Dad would've hated that you've given up. They were always in your corner."

"You don't think I know that? You don't think I know they're up there looking down on me failing at everything? I can't keep a relationship together. I can't keep the two of you out of trouble."

"Gino's not stupid enough to try it again."

I shake my head. "I'm not talking about him." I pin him with a glare. "You said yourself, you're 'making bank', so how is it

78

you're getting paid, Mario? And don't spin me that bullshit about installing security systems." His face drops and he kicks his foot against the floor.

"Yeah, okay, so maybe that wasn't exactly legal, but I ain't doing that shit no more. I swear. Alex and Leo are off to Uni next year, and Skeet's got himself an apprenticeship over at Blackford's Motors." He juts out his chin, tugging his open shirt out. "I got myself an apprenticeship too."

My eyes widen. I had no idea. Here I am wallowing in my own shit while he's pulling himself together without me. "Why didn't you tell me? That's great news."

He shrugs. "You gave up your dreams to look after us, and I know you were down when you heard about Alex and the scholarship. I wasn't gonna rub it in."

Taking him by the shoulders, I level him with my stare. "I didn't give anything up, I just put it on hold. And I'd do it again in a heartbeat if it meant you guys could have the life you deserve. I would never be upset by you succeeding in life. Never."

"And we wouldn't be upset if you followed your dreams either."

I drop my hands from his shoulders. "Why does everyone keep pushing it? Maybe I'm happy writing for *Truly You*."

"What a load of shit. You're so much better than that, Lando, and you know it."

"I don't know anything, and neither do you. I'm happy you've found your place in the world, but don't expect me to run off and leave you two." I turn and swipe my laptop from the bed. "I'm going to get some fresh air."

***

Fresh air took me down the road towards the bustling shopping centre and the little coffee shop Stefan had raved about. Pushing open the door, I'm immediately embraced with the scent of roasted coffee beans and sweet spices. Exposed beams run across the ceiling and the walls look as though they're handmade from clay. There's a real earthy, rustic vibe to the place, and I'm instantly comforted.

Finding a table in the corner, I set my laptop down and take a look at the menu. I order a chai latte with cinnamon and a sticky scroll from the cabinet. It feels good to be out of the house and around people again. I've shut myself away for far too long. Perhaps everyone is right. The boys are getting older now, and as much as I'd like to think they still do, they don't really need me as much anymore. In fact, it's probably the other way around. I've needed them. I've used them as an excuse to hide away. In a way, I think I used Brody as an excuse too. After all, I chose to write the book for him and not me, and when it went pear shaped, as I knew it would, I had another excuse not to follow through.

God, have I been self-sabotaging this whole time? What the hell is wrong with me? I have all these people wanting to help me and I keep pushing them away. I have people who believe in me and want me to succeed, but something is holding me back. Something deep inside won't let me be happy.

I stare out the window, watching strangers go about their daily business, completely oblivious to my inner turmoil. They're all walking around without a care in the world, as if everything they've ever known couldn't be upended and taken away from them. They're all out there living life instead of hiding away.

But how do you go on when the world is so scary? When in a single moment, it can all disappear? How do you find the strength to keep striving forward?

Chapter Fourteen

Stefan

It's almost closing time when the bell above the door jingles and Orlando strides in with his laptop under his arm. The look on his face is one of determination, and I prepare myself for what's about to come. It'll be sad to not have Gino helping me out around here anymore, but it's Orlando I'll miss the most. The way his mouth seems to blurt out what he's thinking before he can stop himself, the way he watches me with his deep brown eyes, the way he grips the back of his neck when he's stressed out, but more importantly, the way he makes my stomach twist in knots when I see him smile.

"G, why don't you go check the back door is locked and gather your things." He looks at Orlando then back to me with a nod before he runs off. He's a smart kid, I know he'll leave us to it.

I round the counter and meet him halfway. "Orlando…"

He holds his hand up to stop me. "Before you say anything, just let me get this out." I drop my hands and nod for him to continue. "After you left, Mario said some things, and it made me get to thinking about everything. Aside from my brothers, you're the only person I've really let in since my parents died. I *thought* I'd let Brody in, but I hadn't, not really. I haven't let anyone in because I've been too afraid of losing them." His voice breaks and a tear rolls down his cheek.

Without thinking, I lift my hand to cup his jaw and wipe away the tear. He leans into my touch with his eyes closed, and it takes everything in me not to pull him into my arms.

"I've been so scared of losing everything, that I've shut myself off from the world, but I don't want to do that anymore." He shakes his head, pulling himself up to stand tall. "I want to live, like really live. I want to find a way to go back to Uni and I want to keep writing." He smiles, taking my hand. "I have you to thank for that. You believed in me before you'd even read anything of mine. I'm still mad at you for reading my story, but I'm also kind of relieved you did." He chuckles. "If you want to read the rest, you can. No more hiding, no more secrets."

I close my eyes, bringing his hand to my chest. "I would love to read the whole thing, but if we're being honest with each other, there's something I need to tell you." My heart hammers in my chest, and I take a deep breath to steady my voice. "This morning, when I read your manuscript... I didn't just read it." I pull my phone out and open up the photos, holding it out to show him. "I took pictures of the first few pages."

"What? Why would you do that?" He steps back, his eyes filling with angry tears. "You were stealing from me?"

"No! Of course not! I mean, not really."

"I can't believe this. I opened up to you, and all this time you were going behind my back?"

"No, it's not like that!"

"Don't." He stalks past me to the back room. "Gino, we're leaving."

"Please, Orlando, it's not what you think."

"I don't care what it is. I was right to hide away. You can't get hurt if you're not putting yourself out there."

I watch him storm out the door with Gino in tow, and I keep watching and waiting for him to turn around and come back. But he doesn't.

Chapter Fifteen

Orlando

My phone is ringing again. It's rung three times every hour since I left *Seconds Away*, and every time I've sent it straight to voicemail. He gave up leaving messages after the fourth try, but he continues to call, nonetheless. I've deleted every message he's sent without reading them first. I don't want to hear what he has to say. I can't believe I was so stupid, letting him in like that. A complete stranger. And to think, he was the one who dragged Gino home after doing something similar. It's almost laughable. A gorgeous guy shows up on my doorstep, offering to help me, pretending that he cares, when really, all he wants is to take what isn't his. I mean really, what did I think would happen? We'd ride off

into the sunset together? Unfortunately, this
isn't one of my romance novels, and the only
knight in shining armour around here is the
one on my kitchen cleaning products. And
even he can't do what he claims.

Maybe a love like my parents had isn't
on the cards for me. Maybe that's why no one
has written the story I want to read; it's just not
possible. I'm chasing something that can never
happen.

I stare at the pages still strewn across my
bed where I left them this afternoon. I should
just throw it all in the bin and be done with it.
Yes, that's what I'll do.

Before I can change my mind, I gather
up the pile shoved between the bed and the
dresser, then start dragging the loose pages
over to the pile. A pop of colour catches my
eye, and I swipe papers side to side until I
uncover what it was; a pamphlet.

A blond-haired, bespectacled guy with a
cheesy grin is on the front, handing a book to a
girl with raven black hair and eyes that sparkle.

The words *"Distance Learning"* are written above them.

Mario.

I shake my head, slapping the pamphlet against my thigh as I look out the door, half expecting to see him standing there with a smug expression on his face, but the hall is empty. After our conversation this morning though, it makes sense that he'd be the one to put it there.

With a sigh, I perch on the edge of my bed and open it up. No harm in looking after all.

"Learn from the comfort of your own home. With Sheaths Distance Learning, you can study at your own pace and even keep working full time. Assignments are sent fortnightly through an online portal, and we have teachers available around the clock for any queries."

I read the whole thing twice, cover to cover. They have a range of literary courses, but the one that stands out to me right now is Creative Writing. The next intake is only three weeks away, and I have to submit an original piece to be accepted. I look back at the crumpled pages on my bed. *Could I submit this? Could I willingly let someone else read it?*

I think back to what Mario said about me giving up my dreams, and he's right. I did give up. I took the easy way out because I was scared. Sheaths Distance Learning could be just what I need to get back on my feet again. I don't need Stefan by my side. As long as I have my brothers and my laptop, I have everything I need.

Chapter Sixteen

Stefan

I gave up calling around ten o'clock last night. It was hopeless trying to sleep, though; all I could see when I closed my eyes was the hurt and the anger in Orlando's eyes before he walked out the door and out of my life. If only he'd given me a chance to explain, to show him I was only trying to help… Ah, who am I kidding? It was a dumb move, and I never should've done it. I should've left it alone for him to decide instead of running in there, guns blazing, as if I have all the answers in the world. When will I learn that not everyone wants to be saved?

Cyan Tayse

Chapter Seventeen

Orlando

I tossed and turned all night. When I first began writing my novel, it was intended for publication. It was always meant to be shared, but now that it's come to the crunch, I'm not sure I can send it through for my enrolment. It's too personal, too raw. And the panic I felt when I saw Stefan reading it... I just don't think I'm ready.

Stefan.

I haven't allowed myself to think of him all weekend, but his presence was missed all the same. He brought life to the place, and not just in me, in everyone. Gino hasn't spoken to me since I told him he was no longer working at *Seconds Away*. I guess he liked the job more than he let on. It's selfish of me to involve him in my dramas, I know that, but I don't think I could face Stefan right now. And deep down, I know I couldn't trust myself around him either. He hurt me more than words can say, but the heart wants what the heart wants, and what mine wants is him.

With a groan, I drag my sorry ass out of bed and down the hall to make a coffee. I need my head clear so I can get something down on paper for this enrolment.

I've spent the weekend checking out the website for Sheaths Distance Learning and reading all the reviews. The more I learn about it, the more I feel it's the right move for me. After all, if you're not moving forward, you're simply standing still and watching life go on around you, and I'm tired of being a bystander in my life.

On a whim, I pull out the frying pan and rustle up some eggs and bacon for the boys. Mario will be off to work soon, and I want to do something nice for him, to show my appreciation for his little nudge in the right direction. He still denies leaving the pamphlet in my room, but I don't believe him.

"Breakfast is ready! Come and get it while it's hot!" I lean back on the counter with my coffee and listen to the sound of pounding feet.

Gino stops in the doorway and Mario almost collides with him. He eyes the plates of food warily. "Okay, who died?"

"What?" I chuckle. "Can't a guy make breakfast for his brothers for no reason?"

"I mean he can, but he wouldn't normally." Gino folds him arms across his chest. "I'm still not talking to you."

Mario scoots around him. "I don't care what the reason, I'm starving!" He grabs a plate and starts loading it up with food. "Thanks, bro."

"You're welcome. Thank you for giving me the push I needed." I take a sip of my coffee. "I'm going to enroll."

"Yeah? That's awesome! But like I said, it wasn't me, honest to God."

My brow furrows at his insistence. The only other person it could've been is… *Stefan.* I shake my head, placing my cup on the counter.

"Nu-uh." Mario points his fork in my direction. "I don't know what went on between you two last week, but you're not using it as an excuse to get out of it. You said you're enrolling, so you are, capiche?"

"Mmhmm." I wave him off. Stefan may have planted the seed, but I'm doing this for me, because it's what *I* want to do.

"I mean it. You need to do this, Lando."

"What are you guys talking about? Enroll in what?" Gino sneaks a piece of bacon and chomps on it.

"Lando's going back to school." Mario puffs out his chest with a grin. "He's gonna get schooled, son."

Gino turns to me for confirmation, and I nod. "What about me?"

"It's an online course so I'll still be here for you whenever you need me." I reach out and ruffle his hair, glad he's finally talking to me. He ducks his head.

"Watch the hair!"

I back up, my hands in the air. "My apologies." I hadn't noticed when he first walked in that he was wearing a shirt and his hair was slicked back with gel. "What are you all dressed up for?"

His eyes flick to the floor as he grips the back of his neck. "Was kinda hoping you'd change your mind and I could go back." He glances up at me, pleading.

"It means a lot to you, doesn't it?"

He nods. "I like earning my money, and Stefan was going to let me work the register this week. He's really cool, Lando. He's teaching me lots, and…" he hesitates, "… I like the way you are together."

"Gino…"

"It's obvious you like him, Lando, and he likes you too. Why can't you just forgive him for whatever he did?"

"It's not that simple."

97

"It's not that hard either." He folds his arms, his eyes narrowing. "When we lost Mum and Dad and you came back home, you were a different person. It was like we lost you too." He looks to Mario who averts his gaze. "Even with Brody you weren't really here. But then Stefan came around and suddenly you were back to the old you. You were out here with us, actually talking and stuff." His eyes fill with tears. "I don't want you to go back to the way you were then." His eyes flick up to the family portrait. "I like having my big brother back."

Rounding the counter, I pull him into my arms, pressing my lips to the top of his head. "I didn't know you felt that way." I reach behind me and draw Mario into our hug. "I'm sorry I haven't been present, guys. I guess I was trying so hard to hold on to everything that I couldn't see what it was doing to me, or you." I pull back, one hand on each of their shoulders. "I'm gonna try harder. I don't want to go back to the way I was either."

"What about Stefan?"

"I know you like him, G. I like him too, but right now, I don't think I can face him. But it was selfish of me to stop you from seeing him, so if you want to go back to work with him, you can."

His face lights up. "Really? Thanks, Lando."

"Now, get this breakfast eaten before it gets cold."

***

"He's picking me up in five minutes. I told him to wait in the car." Gino hovers outside my bedroom door.

"Okay, thanks."

"You sure you don't want to talk to him?"

This kid.

I chuckle, looking up from my laptop. "Yeah, I'm sure." His face drops, but he nods. "Maybe next time." The words are out before I can stop them.

"I'm gonna hold you to that." He grins as he walks back down the hall.

99

Shit. Why'd I have to go and agree to that?

My phone pings from my nightstand, alerting me to a call. My boss's name flashes on the screen, so I pick it up, wondering why he's calling on a Monday when my article isn't due until Wednesday evening.

"Hello?"

"Orlando, hi. Listen, I've been reading this story of yours and I have to say, I'm impressed."

"I'm sorry, what story is this? The piece about the new playground?"

"No, no, not that. The story your friend dropped in..."

No. No, no, no, no, no! He didn't. He wouldn't have.

"... I've been reading it over the weekend, and it blew me away. You've been holding out on me, kid."

"I... uh..."

"Look, like I said to your friend, it's not something I can publish through the magazine, but I know some people who can. I took the

100

liberty of sending a sample to one of my mates up at Segway Publishing, and they're interested in representing you."

My head is spinning. *Did he just say they like my story? An actual publisher likes my story?*

"Wait, what? What did you say?"

He laughs. "It's a lot to take in, isn't it? I always knew you were too good for this place. I've given them your number; I hope that's okay. You should be getting a call sometime soon, and then I expect to receive your resignation."

He's not making any sense. He can't be serious. "Why would I resign?"

"Because they want to offer you a three-book deal. You're going to be spending all your time writing these novels instead of wasting your time on my little magazine. You're an author now." There's a warmth in his voice that fills me with pride.

I'm going to be an author. I like the sound of that. There's just one problem. "The book isn't even finished yet."

"Then you'd better get cracking and finish it, son. You've got a bestseller right there, mark my words."

"I... I don't know what to say... Thank you."

"It's not me you need to thank. Go take that friend of yours out for a drink. I think he deserves one."

I put the phone down just as I hear the front door slam. Gino must be on his way to work. I jolt up, racing to the window to see him climb into Stefan's car before they drive away.

Chapter Eighteen

Stefan

When Gino text me to ask if he could work today, I was surprised. I honestly didn't think I'd see him again after Orlando ignored my attempts to reach out and explain. I can only hope this means he's open to a discussion in the not-too-distant future. I know I'm fooling myself, but my eyes keep finding their way back to my phone every few minutes, hoping to see his name pop up on the screen.

"For God's sake, this is ridiculous." I snatch it off the counter and march out back to shove it in the drawer of my desk. Out of sight, out of mind.

The bell over the door jingles, and I get a hit of that delectable coffee fragrance. "That was quick." I'd sent Gino out to *Roasted Beans* only a few minutes before. "You're a lifesaver, G, I could really use a caffeine hit..." Words fail me as I step through the door and find Orlando standing there with two cups in his hand.

"I hope you don't mind." He places the cups on the counter. "I ran into Gino on my way here and told him to give us a few minutes." I don't move for fear of sending him running again. "Or I can just go..." He hooks a thumb over his shoulder.

"No." I step forward cautiously, holding my hand up to stop him. "Don't go. Please stay."

A slow smile forms on his lips, and his cheeks pinken just a touch as he forces out a breath. "I was hoping you'd say that."

"I would never send you away." His eyes flick up to mine then down to where his hands idly touch things on the counter. "Orlando, about the other day..."

"I know," he interrupts.

"You know?"

104

He nods. "I know what you did."

I let out the breath I'd been holding. "I'm sorry. I never should've gone behind your back like that."

"No, you shouldn't have, but I'm glad you did."

"I know, it was so wrong of me and… wait, what?"

His eyes light up as he grins like the cat who got the cream. "I've been offered a book deal."

"You…" I brace myself against the counter.

"I know, I couldn't believe it either, but they're sending me a contract. They want me to finish the book *and* write more. They're going to publish my book."

"Wow." I shake my head. "I mean, wow! That's great news, Orlando! I'm so proud of you!" I round the corner of the counter and throw my arms around him, pulling him in tight and breathing him in. "I knew they'd love it." When I pull back, his eyes glisten with tears.

"I owe it all to you, Stefan. I never would've had the courage to show it to anyone, but you believed in me when I couldn't believe in myself. I'm so sorry I thought anything different."

I shake my head. "You have nothing to apologise for. I went about it all wrong."

He laughs. "We make a good pair, don't we? Act first, ask questions later."

I bring my hand up to cup his cheek and wipe away his tears. "We sure do." Biting my lip, I press my forehead to his. "Where do we go from here?"

"I don't know about you, but I think you guys should kiss and make up." Gino stands in the doorway with his hand holding the bell in place and a goofy grin on his face.

"He has a good point." I look into Orlando's eyes, asking permission.

"That he does," he whispers, his breath mingling with mine as he leans in. With a low growl, I press my lips to his, sweeping my hand around to grip the back of his head, holding him in place as the kiss deepens.

Gino clears his throat. "Ah, maybe I'll come back in five." The bell jingles as he closes the door behind him.

Pressing myself against him, I trail my hand down his back to find something sticking out from his back pocket. I pull back with a questioning look.

"Oh, ah." He reaches back and pulls out folded sheets of paper. "I thought maybe you'd like to read the next bit?"

"Really? You want me to?" My fingers curl around the pages, knowing just how much this means to him.

"I want you to." He grins, pulling his lip between his teeth. "I was kinda hoping you could help me finish it."

I wave my hand through the air as if reading an announcement. "A secondhand love story for our time."

He laughs, slapping a hand to my chest. "Ah, no. I was thinking more the *greatest* love story of our time."

"Right, so no pressure then." I roll my eyes.

"Not at all. Like a wise man once told me; it's in you, it's in me, it's in all of us." He closes his eyes, one hand across his chest.

Placing the manuscript on the counter, I wrap my arms around his waist. "Wow, that's beautiful. He sounds like a keeper, this wise man of yours."

"I think so, but he hasn't answered the question yet." He tilts his head, pursing his lips.

"You even have to ask?" I tug him closer, my lips brushing against his. "I want to help you finish the story. I just have one amendment."

"What's that?"

"It won't just be the greatest love story of our time; it'll be the greatest love story of *all* time."

Acknowledgements

First and foremost, I have to thank my friend and proofreader, Trina. Thank you for always having my back and making sure everything I write makes sense. Couldn't do this without you!

A huge thank you to my ARC team for reading and reviewing. You guys are awesome!

And of course, a huge thank you to you, the reader. Without you, I couldn't do this job I love so much. Thank you for taking a chance on me and my books. I appreciate each and every one of you.

Cyan xxx

Other Books by Cyan Tayse

Pocket Rocket Novellas

Have you Ever…?
Blank Canvas
A Gift to Remember

Brief Encounters Novellas

Thick as Thieves
Secondhand Lover

About Cyan Tayse

Cyan Tayse is the pen name of a multi-genre author based in New Zealand. After a lot of coaxing from friends, she decided to embark on a journey of discovery. Yes, that's right, she embraced her desire to write things a little different to her usual, thus the Pocket Rocket and Brief Encounters novellas were born.

Cyan can often be found lurking on social media, and she loves to hear from fellow authors and readers.

www.cyantayse.weebly.com
https://www.facebook.com/CyanTayse

Lightning Source UK Ltd.
Milton Keynes UK
UKHW020434031121
393296UK00011B/804